Snoopy: Flying Ace to the Rescue

LITTLE SIMON
An imprint of Simon & Schuster Children's Publishing Division
1230 Avenue of the Americas, New York, New York 10020
Copyright © 2002 by United Feature Syndicate, Inc. All rights reserved.
PEANUTS is a registered trademark of United Feature Syndicate, Inc.
LITTLE SIMON is a registered trademark of Simon & Schuster, Inc., and associated
colophon is a trademark of Simon & Schuster, Inc.
All rights reserved, including the right of reproduction in whole or in part in any form.
Manufactured in China
ISBN-13: 978-1-4169-1381-8
ISBN-10: 1-4169-1381-5

Snoopy: Flying Ace
to the Rescue

Based on the comic strips by Charles M. Schulz
Adapted by Darice Bailer
Art adapted by Peter and Nick LoBianco

LITTLE SIMON
New York   London   Toronto   Sydney

Lucy looked up at Snoopy
sitting on his doghouse.
"What you need is a real job,"
she said.

I do have a real job, thought Snoopy.
He put on his helmet, his scarf,
and his goggles.
He was a World War I Flying Ace.
It was time for him to fight
the great German pilot—
the Red Baron!

Snoopy dusted off his
Sopwith Camel airplane.
"I am on to you, Red Baron!"
he shouted.
Lucy rolled her eyes.
"That World War I act
   drives me crazy," she said.

Later that morning
Lucy, Snoopy, and Charlie Brown
were walking to school.
"I think you need a good dog,"
Lucy told Charlie Brown.
"But I have a dog," said Charlie Brown.
Lucy nodded. "I said a *good* dog."
Snoopy frowned at Lucy.

While Charlie Brown was in school
Snoopy walked down the runway.
"Good morning, chaps!"
he said to his crew.
He shook their hands
and climbed into the cockpit.
"Wish me luck," he said.

"The World War I Flying Ace
  is zooming through the air,"
  Snoopy said.
"I must bring the Red Baron down!
  Go, Sopwith Camel, go!"

Snoopy spotted the Red Baron's plane!
It was straight ahead.
"There he is!" Snoopy cried,
shaking his fist.
"I'll get you, Red Baron!
This time you are mine!"

"Take that!" Snoopy shouted.
"And that!"
  Snoopy thought that he had
  the Red Baron for sure.
"Nyahh, nyahh!" Snoopy said.
"You cannot hit me!"

POW!
A snowball hit Snoopy
right in the head!
Snoopy did not see Linus
behind a tree.

"Great Scott!" Snoopy cried.
"The Red Baron hit my plane!"

"Curse you, Red Baron!"
Snoopy said.
Then he sniffed the air.
Smoke rose up around him.
His plane was on fire!

"I must bail out!" Snoopy cried.
Snoopy leaped from his cockpit
and landed . . .

Plop!
. . . right in his dog dish!
Charlie Brown looked at Snoopy.
"World War I pilots do not land
in dog dishes," he said.
"Rats," said Snoopy.
What was his dog dish doing
behind enemy lines?

Snoopy ran away from his Sopwith Camel.
"I am hurt!" Snoopy cried.
"I must find a first-aid station fast."

"There it is!" Snoopy said.
"Ah—and a beautiful nurse is coming."
Marcie held Snoopy's paw.
"I see you tripped over your
supper dish again," she said.
Marcie taped on a bandage.

After he was bandaged
Snoopy dashed off.
I'm trapped in the middle
of no-man's-land, he thought.
I must get through
that barbed-wire fence.

Snoopy hopped over the fence . . .
and right into the girls' jump rope!
"Is that your dog, Charlie Brown?"
Linus asked, pointing at Snoopy.
"I think he's lost his mind!"

Charlie Brown wished he had a dog
like other dogs . . .
a dog that chased balls
or sticks or cars.
Why did *his* dog have to
chase the Red Baron?

"Good Grief!" Charlie Brown cried
as Snoopy ran to his plane.
Linus was run down too.
Linus lifted his head.
"Why don't you try raising
goldfish or something?"
Charlie Brown just sighed.

Snoopy patched up his plane
and took off for the sky.
"Chocks away!" Snoopy cried.

Later, Charlie Brown and Linus
kicked a football back and forth.
Snoopy watched the ball
sail over his head.
"Good grief!" Snoopy cried.
"It is a German plane!"
BONK!
The football smacked Snoopy
right in the head!

"Aaaugh!" Snoopy cried.
"The Red Baron got me!
  He's right on my tail!"
  Snoopy lay dazed on the ground.
"It was a cowardly attack!" he cried.
"He hit me from behind!"

27

Charlie Brown brought Snoopy
his dinner later.
But Snoopy thought
the round-headed kid was a spy.
He threw a stone at him.
KLUNK!
Dog food splattered all over!
"I can't stand it," said Charlie Brown.

On the next mission
a cloud rolled in overhead.
It started to rain.
"Come back!" Linus yelled at Snoopy.
"You can't fly in the rain!"

"Rats!" Snoopy said.
Snoopy landed his plane
and raced across the field.
BAM! BAM! BAM!
He kicked Charlie Brown's door.

Snoopy slipped into
Charlie Brown's bed.
"I smell a wet pilot,"
Charlie Brown said.